Hello Sun!

To everyone who loves the Sun

Carolrhoda Books, Inc.
A division of Lerner Publishing Group
241 First Avenue North
Minneapolis, MN 55401 U.S.A.

Website address: www.lernerbooks.com

For more information about Hans Wilhelm, please visit: www.hanswilhelm.com

Library of Congress Cataloging-in-Publication Data

Wilhelm, Hans, 1945-
Hello sun! / written and illustrated by Hans Wilhelm.
p. cm.
Summary: Upon feeling a sunbeam for the first time, a young hedgehog decides to build a tree house so that he can see the sun itself, and, despite teasing and a bet with a wily fox, he finds a way to get the job done.
ISBN: 1-57505-348-9 (lib. bdg. : alk. paper)
[1. Hedgehogs – Fiction. 2. Forest animals – Fiction. 3. Sun – Fiction.] I. title.
PZ7.W64816 He 2003
[E]–dc21 2002151966

Manufactured in the United States of America
1 2 3 4 5 6 – DP – 08 07 06 05 04 03

Hello Sun!

by Hans Wilhelm

Carolrhoda Books, Inc. • Minneapolis

Early one morning, Charlie Rabbit, Weasel, and Badger peeked through the bushes and saw an unusual sight—

Quentin, the little hedgehog, stood on his hind legs, bathed in the light of a sunbeam. Quentin was never awake during the day! He was so happy he felt like singing.

Little light, with all your might,
You help the flowers grow.
You make me cheerful every day.
You warm my little toe . . .

"That's no 'little light,'" laughed Charlie Rabbit. "That's the sun. It's bigger than the whole forest."

"If it's so big, why can't we see it?" asked Quentin.

"The trees block out the sun and only let a few sunbeams through. That's why the forest is so dark, silly!" replied Charlie.

"But what does the sun *look* like?" asked Quentin.

"I don't know," said Charlie, "and I don't care. As long as I have green to nibble and flowers to smell, I'm happy. Why do you care anyway? You're a night creature!"

But Quentin was not satisfied. He wanted to know all about the sun, so he decided to visit wise old Owl.

"Imagine a giant, juicy berry," explained Owl. "That's what the sun looks like when it rises every morning. At midday, the sun looks like a big flower growing in the sky. And in the evening, it disappears behind the mountains like a huge ball of fire. The sun is most beautiful when seen from above the treetops."

The more Quentin heard about the sun, the more he wanted to see it for himself. Suddenly, he had an idea.

"I'm going to build a tree house at the top of the tallest tree. That way, I can see the sun every day."

Quentin went home to plan his tree house. When Fox heard about Quentin's idea, he came up with a wicked plan of his own.

"I hear you're building a tree house," Fox said. "Aren't you a little small to do that?"

"I am not," said Quentin.

"Really?" Fox paused. "How about a little bet? If you finish it in three days, I will cook up a feast for your tree house-warming party."

"But if you lose," Fox continued, "you'll have to clean up my messy burrow."

"It's a deal," said Quentin.

Fox's mouth watered. Hedgehogs were his favorite dinner, but they were difficult to catch because of their sharp spines. Soon, Quentin would be cleaning up his burrow and Fox would easily be able to throw him into a pot of boiling water. "What a delicious dinner it will be," thought Fox.

Early the next morning, Quentin went to see Beaver.

"Would you be interested in a little trade?" he asked. "If I collect twigs for your dam, would you cut some wood for my tree house?"

"I could use a change of pace," said Beaver. "It's a deal. For a bundle of twigs, I'll have all your wood cut by tonight."

Quentin finished the job so quickly, he was able to spend the entire day fishing. When Fox passed by and saw Quentin, he laughed to himself. Obviously, Quentin had not started to build his tree house.

Charlie and his friends stopped by and teased Quentin, "Guess you gave up on your tree house." Then, they started singing,

Quentin is a bragger,
Who longs to see the sun.
He wants to build a tree house,
But hasn't yet begun!

Quentin ignored them. Just two more days until he would finally see the sun.

The next day, Quentin went to see Squirrel.

"Would you be interested in a little trade?" he asked. "If I collect nuts for you today, would you climb high up in the trees and build the walls for my tree house?"

"Well, I am a little tired of looking for nuts," said Squirrel. "It's a deal. For a basket of acorns, I'll help build your tree house."

Quentin gathered acorns quickly. When his basket was full, he decided to take a rest.

Fox was surprised to see Quentin napping. "He's making it easier for me than I thought," he laughed.

Charlie, Weasel, and Badger soon came along singing,

Quentin is a bragger,
Who longs to see the sun.
He wants to build a tree house,
But hasn't yet begun!

Quentin did not respond. In the warm light of a sun ray, he dreamed about seeing the sun. Just one more day.

The next morning, Quentin went to see the Robins.

"Would you be interested in a little trade?" he asked. "If I baby-sit your little ones today, would you fly high up in the trees and build the roof for my tree house?"

"We sure could do with a break from those little rascals," sighed Mrs. Robin. "It's a deal. If you watch our children all day, we will finish your roof by tonight."

Quentin spent all day telling stories to the little Robins.

Fox was pleased when he saw Quentin sitting in the Robins' nest.

"Tomorrow I'll have won my bet," he said to himself, "and then I shall have the finest hedgehog supper I've ever had!"

Soon Charlie and his friends started to tease Quentin again.

Quentin is a bragger,
Who longs to see the sun.
He wants to build a tree house,
But hasn't yet begun!

They sang their silly song again and again, until the Robins flew down and chirped, "**YOUR TREE HOUSE IS FINISHED!**"

"Finished?" gasped Charlie.

"Yes," said Quentin. "Come look!"

There it was—a beautiful tree house high up in the branches of an old oak tree. Everyone was impressed, especially Charlie.

"Wait a minute," Fox said suddenly. "How are you going to get all the way up there?"

"Oh no!" Quentin hadn't thought about that.

"You have lost our little bet," said Fox. "I shall be expecting you in the morning at my place."

Fox left with a big grin on his face.

Quentin felt awful.

Quietly, Charlie asked, "Would you be interested in a little trade?"

"What do you mean?" asked Quentin.

"If Badger, Weasel, and I help you build a rope ladder," said Charlie, "could we climb up to your tree house and have a look at the sun, too?"

"It's a deal!" exclaimed Quentin.

In the light of many dancing fireflies, the forest animals built a long rope ladder. It took them all night. When the first sunbeams broke through the thick forest, they were finally done. Everyone was excited. Soon they would see something that very few forest animals had ever seen.

Quentin was the first to climb up the ladder. His heart was beating loudly. When he reached the top . . .

...the sun welcomed him with the warmest light!

"Hello Sun!" shouted Quentin.

The others joined him and greeted the sun, too. Then Charlie started to sing,

Great big sun, you are so bright.
You bathe us in your glow.
You guide us on our merry way
And warm us head to toe.

All day long, the animals came to admire Quentin's tree house. They brought flowers and gifts and a huge appetite. Fox served up quite a feast!

Together they watched the sun. It was as bright and beautiful as Quentin dreamed it would be. He wouldn't have traded this moment for anything!